These promises are especially for

Coleby Alexander Rempel

With love from

Grandma Martens

*The Lord…is pleased with those
who do what they promise.*

P R O V E R B S   1 2 : 2 2

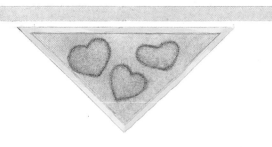

GRANDMOTHER'S
Book of Promises

WRITTEN BY KAREN HILL   ILLUSTRATED BY DAVID CLAR

WATERBROOK
PRESS

GRANDMOTHER'S BOOK OF PROMISES
PUBLISHED BY WATERBROOK PRESS
2375 Telstar Drive, Suite 160
Colorado Springs, Colorado 80920
A division of Random House, Inc.

All Scripture quotations are from *The International Children's Bible,
New Century Version,* © 1986, 1988 by Word Publishing,
Nashville, TN 37214. Used by permission. All rights reserved.

ISBN 1-57856-579-0

Library of Congress Cataloging-in-Publication Data
Hill, Karen, 1947–
    Grandmother's book of promises / written by Karen Hill ; illustrated by David Clar.
        p. cm.
    Summary: A grandmother promises to skip stones, dunk cookies, and love her
grandchild in every way forever.
    ISBN 1-57856-221-X
    [1. Grandmothers—Fiction. 2. Promises—Fiction. 3. Rabbits—Fiction. 4. Christian
life—Fiction. 5. Stories in rhyme.] I. Clar, David, ill. II. Title.

PZ8.3.H55114 Gr 2000
[E]—dc21   00-043255

Printed in the United States of America
2001

10 9 8 7 6 5 4 3 2 1

For Shelby
What a precious gift you are!
—K.H.

Every perfect gift is from God.

JAMES 1:17

Dedicated with love to Corinne,
who keeps her promises.
—D.C.

Come, Grandchild, come!
Please take a look —
I have something for you;
it's your own special book!
Pages of promises
straight from my heart.
We'll read them together.
Are you ready? Let's start!

I will always love you
just the way you are.
I'll be your biggest fan;
you'll be my favorite star.
Even if your toes are chubby,
even if your clothes are funny,
I'll love you every single hour,
on rainy days or when it's sunny.

We'll plant seeds and watch them grow.
We'll feed them and weed them, and soon we'll know—
Flowers will sprout and start to bloom,
then into a vase to brighten the room.

We'll praise God together
for all that he's done.
We'll count every blessing
under the sun.
We'll thank him for family,
home, friendships, and fun.
We'll name them out loud,
every little last one.

Here's a promise for your tummy:
The food I cook will be—oh!—so yummy.
Rabbit-shaped pancakes with raisin eyes,
cookies and cocoa and maybe some fries!
All kinds of milkshakes to make our
tongues shiver.
But I promise we'll never, ever eat liver!

I Also Promise to...

Keep track of your height on my kitchen door.

Keep your pictures on my fridge.

Always laugh at your jokes.

Help you clean up your messes.

Brush your hair and pour bubbles into your bath.

Hold these promises deep in your heart,
and remember my love for you right from the start!

When we have a crazy-dazy day,
upside down is the way to play.
I'll call you "Granny" and you'll call me you,
I'll wear my shirt backward for fun—you will too!

We'll take imaginary trips
in a cloth house made of quilts.
First it's a plane! Then it's a boat!
We'll buzz the clouds,
   and on the sea we'll float.

I'll never say, "Hurry up! Move along!"
I'll slow down with you and take routes that are long.
We won't ever rush. We'll take our sweet time,
exploring together the wonders we'll find.

We'll chase lightning bugs together
in the toasty summer weather.
We'll catch them in our hands
and feel their wings like little fans.
We'll put our fireflies in a jar
and watch their light from near and far.
After a while we'll let them go
and cheer them on as they glow, glow, glow.

I Also Promise to...

Teach you how to whistle.

Show you how to skip stones on water.

Teach you to fly a kite.

Share with you the fun of dunking cookies in milk.

Teach you all the silly songs I know!

Hold these promises deep in your heart,
and remember my love for you right from the start!

On cool, clear nights we'll count the stars
and planet hop from here to Mars.
On a make-believe cloud through the sky
  we'll zoom
and stop for a chat with the man in the moon.
We'll eat comet ice cream before we land
and dance to the tunes of the Galaxy Band.

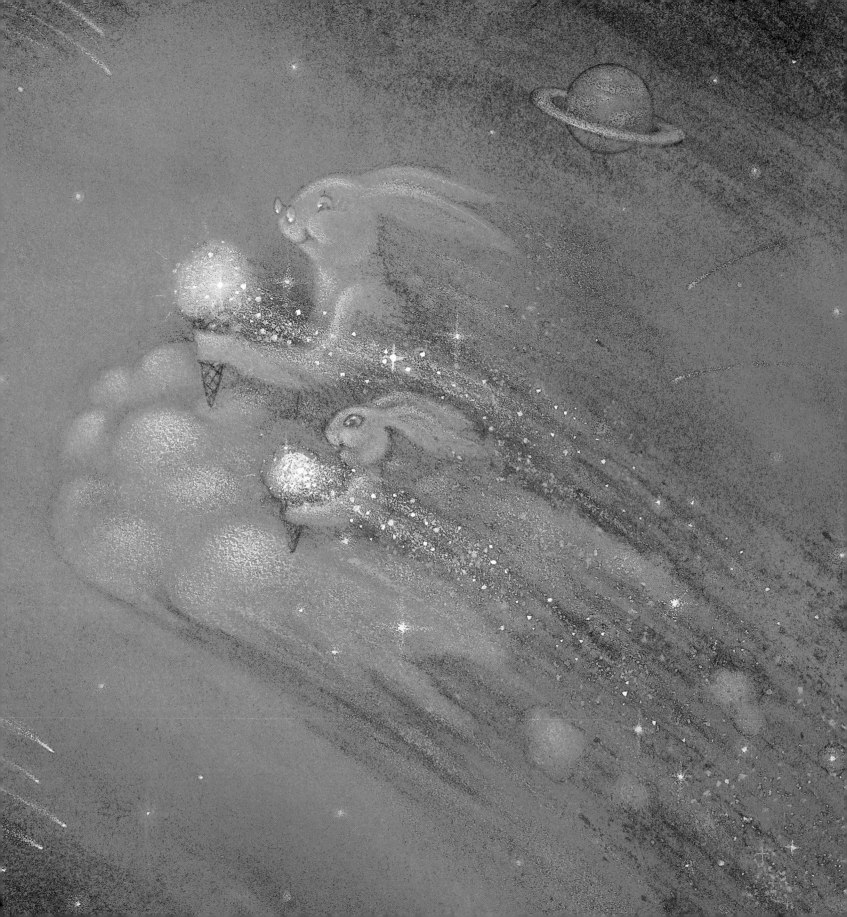

We'll have a sleepover, just you and me.
We'll sing silly songs, watch a little TV.
We'll snack on goodies, and before we're done,
we'll read stacks of books and have loads of fun.

If bedtime makes you cry,
I'll sit by your bed till your tears are dry.
I promise—if you're scared at night,
I'll sing you songs and leave on the light.

Squirt you with the hose on hot summer days.
   (You can squirt me too!)
Make paper snowflakes with you and pretend
   we're shivering.
Take flashlight walks together before bedtime.
Draw pictures together in the sand.
Save bread crusts so we can feed the birds.

Hold these promises deep in your heart,
and remember my love for you right from the start!

On a starry night long ago,
Jesus was born (I'm sure you know).
So let's have a party to celebrate,
with a Christmas tree and a birthday cake!
We'll sip cocoa and trim the tree
as we sing about the first Christmas Eve.

For quiet time we'll snuggle together
in a big old chair, whatever the weather.
We'll read awhile, and when we're done,
I'll tell you stories of when I was young.

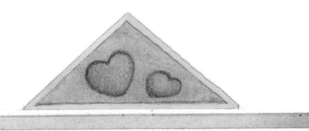

I promise to pray for you each single day.
I'll help you and love you in every way.
I'll care for you always, with all of my heart,
forever and ever, right from the start.
You're special,
   you're AWESOME,
      you're one of a kind!
Best of all, dear Grandchild, you are mine
   for all time!

Here are my own special promises for you...

Wise Things Your Grandma Told You.

You are special.

Manners matter.

Treat others the way you want to be treated.

Your life can be what you want it to be.

Take the days one day at a time.

Always play fair.

Count your blessings, not your troubles.

Don't put limits on yourself.

It's never to late.

Put things back where you found them.

Decisions are to important to leave to chance.

...and extra blessings to go with you into life.

Reach for the stars.

Clean up after yourself.

Nothing wastes more energy than worrying.

The longer you carry a problem, the heavier it gets.

Say "I'm sorry" when you've hurt someone.

A little love goes a long way.

Friendship is always a good investment.

Don't take things to seriously.

Trust in the Lord with all your heart.

Love one another, for love is of God.

The Lord bless you and keep you while we are absent one from another.

Hold these promises deep in your heart,

and remember my love for you right from the start! Love always, your Grandma Martens